ONLY A PIGEON

BY *Jane* AND *Christopher Kurtz*   ILLUSTRATED BY *E. B. Lewis*

Simon & Schuster Books for Young Readers

SIMON & SCHUSTER BOOKS FOR YOUNG READERS An imprint of Simon & Schuster Children's Publishing Division, 1230 Avenue of the Americas, New York, New York 10020. Text copyright © 1997 by Jane and Christopher Kurtz. Illustrations copyright © 1997 by E. B. Lewis. All rights reserved including the right of reproduction in whole or in part in any form. SIMON & SCHUSTER BOOKS FOR YOUNG READERS is a trademark of Simon & Schuster. Book design by Paul Zakris. The text for this book is set in 18-point Garamond. The illustrations are rendered in watercolor.
Printed and bound in the United States of America. First Edition 10 9 8 7 6 5 4 3 2 1
LIBRARY OF CONGRESS CATALOGING-IN-PUBLICATION DATA
Kurtz, Jane.
   Only a pigeon / Jane Kurtz [and Christopher Kurtz] ; illustrated by E. B. Lewis. — 1st edition
           p.   cm.
   Summary: Ondu-ahlem carefully trains his pigeons and prepares them for the day when he and other Ethiopian boys test the homing instinct and loyalty of their precious birds.
   ISBN 0-689-80077-0
   [1. Homing pigeons—Fiction. 2. Pigeons—Fiction. 3. Ethiopia—Fiction.]
I. Kurtz, Christopher. II. Lewis, Earl B., ill. III. Title.
P27.K96260n 1997   [E]—dc20   95-44056

To Andualem "Mamoosh" Minale,
who showed me it's never just a pigeon
—C. K.

For Chris, who has taught me so much about
pigeons and life—and who makes me laugh
—J. K.

To Earl C. Smith, my grandfather,
who taught me that today is the future
—E. B. L.

In Ethiopia,
a land of ancient churches and castles,
of mountains and waterfalls,
of coffee beans roasting on the fire,
the sun rises over the city of Addis Ababa,
over the palaces of former kings,
over beautiful houses of stone and brick,
with electric lights and televisions
and water that runs out of the faucets,
and over small houses where the children
own almost nothing, sometimes only a pigeon.

In the small houses, early morning smoke—smelling like sweet eucalyptus—trails out of the cracks where the roof meets the wall. Women bend over fires, warming a little soup for the morning meal. People already walk along the road on their way to church or work. Children call to each other, their voices high and clear.

One Friday, in one of the small houses, Ondu-ahlem rises from the floor where he shares a mat and blanket with his two younger brothers. As he hurries to pull on his pants and jacket, he watches the other boys move closer to each other for warmth. The smoke from his mother's fire stings his eyes and he steps out of the house quickly.

Impatient pigeons grunt and chuckle, climbing the wire mesh of their coop until he opens the door. Baby pigeons begin to squeal. Larger birds explode out the door with a loud clapping of wings. Ondu-ahlem knows, without counting, which birds are not yet out. Only when the last birds are flushed from their hiding places can he relax. The night holds many dangers. As he turns away from the coop, he stoops to look with fear at something on the ground. Footprints. A *shele mit-mot,* or mongoose, has been around the coop during the night.

He reaches into a bag and speckles grain onto the bare ground, and his pigeons flutter down noisily to eat. Gubsima, Remedi, Grees: each bird has a name. He watches for signs of sickness or a hurt leg or wing. Going back to the cage, he gently lifts out a young bird whose parents were killed one night last week. He feeds the bird moistened grain from his mouth. But he never forgets to watch the corners and edges of the fence for the skinny cats who sometimes lurk there.

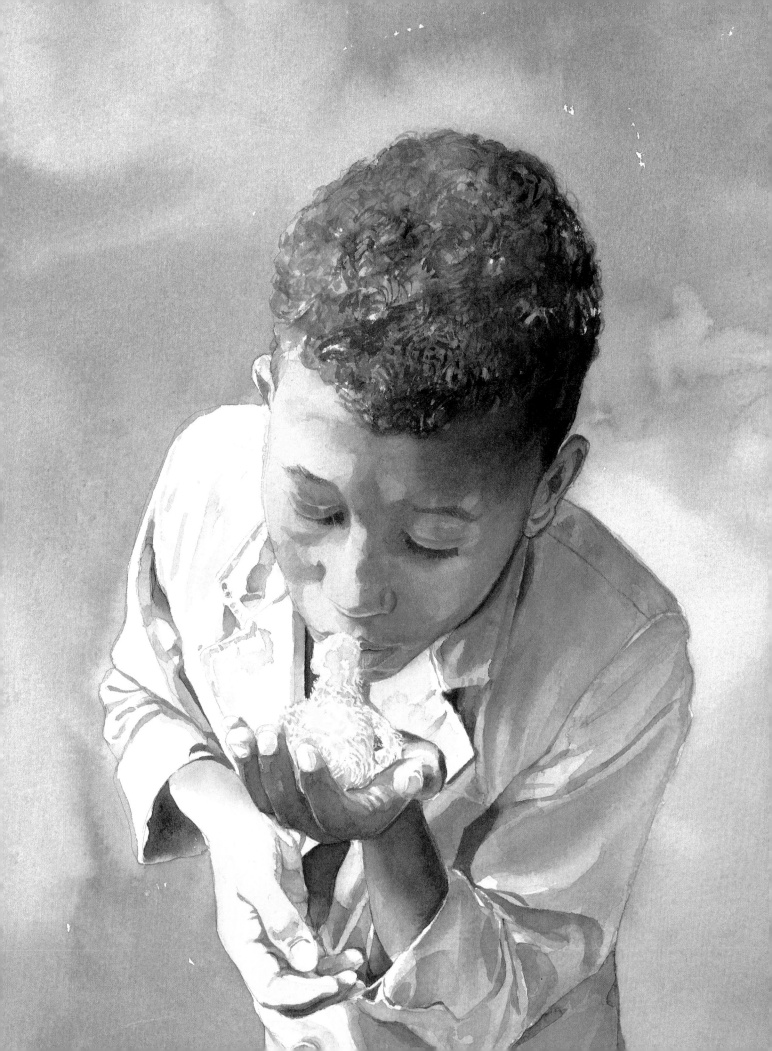

Chinkay, his favorite pigeon, returns to the cage to sit on a pair of eggs. The bird grunts a warning when Ondu-ahlem gets too close. The boy admires the bird's bravery—he will not leave his nest even when Ondu-ahlem reaches under him. His wings strike the boy's hand like tiny boxing gloves. Ondu-ahlem draws out one of the eggs, strokes it gently with his thumb, and then holds it to his cheek to feel its warmth. When he hears a soft ticking, he smiles. The baby bird will peck its way out within a few days. He carefully puts the egg back.

Ondu-ahlem must be at school by eight o'clock and he has three miles to walk. "Mamoosh," he calls to his brother, who is just now getting up. "See to it that nothing happens to these eggs." The younger boy emerges sleepily from the dark doorway. Ondu-ahlem puts a hand on his brother's shoulder. "If no harm comes to them today, I might let you come with me tomorrow."

"Did they hatch yet?" asks the boy.

"Soon," Ondu-ahlem whispers, and his eyes shine with the thought. "Before next week is gone, I think."

He runs off to school, where he spends his mornings in a class with eighty other students reciting the lessons and copying paragraphs from the board, carefully shaping the Amharic letters. During recess some of the boys play a soccer game with a ball they have made by wrapping plastic bags tightly together.

At noon, the afternoon students arrive and Ondu-ahlem must head home even though he would rather stay and study longer. The classrooms would be too crowded if school lasted all day. As soon as he gets home, he goes immediately to the birds. He notices his brother watching him. "Tomorrow," Ondu-ahlem promises. He smiles to see his brother's excitement and then picks up the tools of his trade: polish, a blackened cloth, a brush in the well-worn carrying box with the smooth handle. He will spend the afternoon on the sidewalks, shining the shoes of businessmen, who give him one or two coins in payment. When he is hungry he buys a handful of roasted chickpeas from a peddler younger than himself.

On the way home that evening, he walks through the *markato*. Tired from the long day's work, he hurries past the pyramids of hot, bright spices, past the piles of onions and garlic and other vegetables, past the

tailors sewing on their machines in a long line. Later he will use some of his coins to buy things the family needs. For now, he spends a little money on grain for his pigeons.

Early the next morning, Ondu-ahlem nudges Mamoosh awake. "Is it time?" Mamoosh asks sleepily.

"Yes," Ondu-ahlem says. "Hurry." He and Mamoosh run to where his friends have gathered at a rusty iron gate. The boys talk about the price of grain and trade stories of *selah,* the dusty brown hawk who swoops down to carry off unprotected pigeons. Two or three boys have special birds with them. Ondu-ahlem takes Chinkay from Mamoosh's hands and holds the pigeon out, spreading his wings carefully to display the colors. A beautiful bird—and loyal. Another spreads the wings of his own bird. The game has begun.

The group walks to a point equally far from the homes of each bird. Mamoosh and the other younger boys laugh and run ahead. Older boys make their predictions. The pigeons are held chest to chest. Someone counts: *"Ond, hoo-let, sohst,"* and the birds are thrown into the air. Wild birds for a few moments, they clap their wings with a *kwaa, kwaa, kwaa* sound in the cool morning air. Then they circle once and head for home.

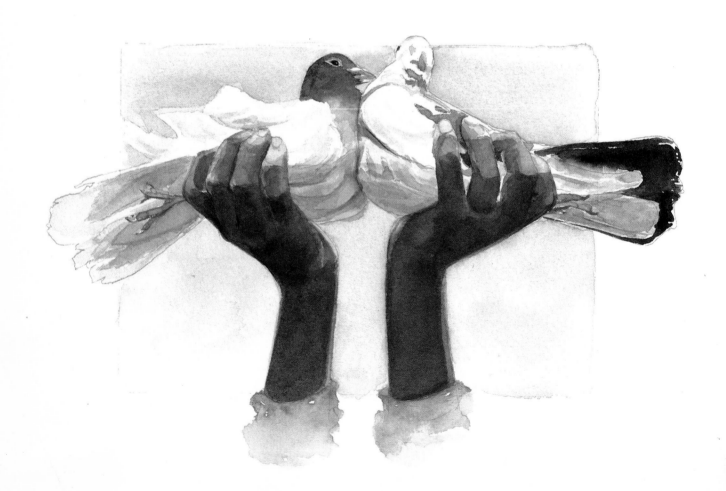

Pointing and shouting and whistling encouragement, the boys begin to run. When Ondu-ahlem sees his house, he slows down, his breath loud in his ears. He puts his hand into his pocket and feels a few choice kernels of corn there. If the other boy's bird has followed his, he will feed it to make it feel at home. But what if the other bird has coaxed away his own? If Chinkay does not return, his favorite bird will never again see his cage. Ondu-ahlem feels Mamoosh clutching the back of his jacket.

They walk silently to the house and stare up at the tin roof. Suddenly both boys begin to shout with excitement. Chinkay is there, strutting calmly. Even though Chinkay did not manage to lure the other boy's bird away, Ondu-ahlem whispers soft words and feeds him the kernels of corn as a reward for coming home.

Night in Addis Ababa is cold. In the small houses, children sleep deeply, wrapped in a *gahbi* or snuggled together with brothers and sisters for warmth. But in parts of the city, the night rustles. Remembering the mongoose tracks, Ondu-ahlem has piled up some small rocks he can throw if there is any danger. Now he sits near the cage, watching, with his rocks beside him. Tiredness tugs at him, but he shakes it off as long as he can. Finally he slumps against the wall and lets sleep cover him like a blanket.

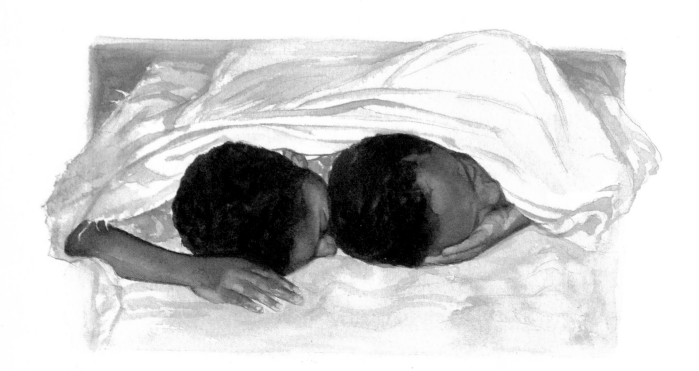

Wild flapping jerks him awake. A *shele mit-mot* has slipped into the cage. The mongoose's black fur is invisible in the darkness—the white feathers that flash inside the wire mesh are the only sign the killer is striking. Ondu-ahlem shouts and grabs a rock. When he reaches the cage, the intruder is gone. Was he in time? Did the mongoose kill any of his birds? He dares not open the door. Even tomorrow, the birds will have to stay inside or fear will scatter them forever. Biting his lip, he stands in the darkness, surrounded by the soft, musty scent of the cage. Did Chinkay come home from the race, only to be killed by a mongoose? *"I-zo, i-zo."* He speaks softly to the frightened birds as he begins to repair the hole the mongoose has made. One of the pigeons may be wounded or missing, but he can't tell in the darkness.

When the first light touches the horizon, Ondu-ahlem is already standing by his cage, straining to see, counting each bird. His breath catches on the fear in his throat. He counts them again, just to make sure. Yes, for one more day the birds are all safe. He reaches through the wire mesh to gently stroke a few feathers and thinks of the eggs almost ready to hatch.

Some may say it is only a pigeon. But his heart says it is something proud and beautiful, something that kisses the sky.

Glossary

CHINKAY (CHIN-kay): black head

GAHBI (GAH-bee): a thick, warm cloak

GREES (Grees): the color of brown water

GUBSIMA (Gub-SIM-ah): a mottled gray and brown color

HOO-LET (hoo-LET): two

I-ZO (EYE-zoh): Don't be afraid

MARKATO (mar-KAH-toh): an outdoor marketplace

OND (ond): one

ONDU-AHLEM (on-du-AH-lem): One World

REMEDI (REH-muh-dee): gray

SELAH (SEE-lah): hawk

SHELE MIT-MOT (shell-luh MIT-mot): mongoose

SOHST (sohst): three

AUTHOR'S NOTE

An Ethiopian boy like Ondu-ahlem would start pigeon-raising by buying a pigeon or two from another boy who raises pigeons. Boys build their flocks through breeding or sending one of their birds up to lure an unattached pigeon back to the cage.

Pigeons begin life with a homing instinct that guides them back to their homes after flight. Some pigeons, bred for their homing ability, will return to the place of their birth in spite of huge separations of time or distance. Other breeds can be more easily persuaded to adopt a new home. A bird can be lured to a new cage if it mates with a bird already settled in the cage. Sometimes the boys pluck a new pigeon's flight feathers or keep it in the cage for a while. By the time the new pigeon is flying free again, it may well return consistently to the new nesting spot.

Training a pigeon to be a "homer" is a matter of simply using the bird's instinct, making the home as attractive as possible, strengthening the bird's ability to fly long distances, and letting the bird become familiar with landmarks farther and farther away from its home. In fact the homing instinct of some pigeons is so impressive that they seem to need no familiar landmarks in order to return home. It's still a mystery to scientists how the birds get their bearings when set free miles from home in unfamiliar terrain, having been carried in an enclosed box. Some scientists theorize that the pigeons make use of the location of the sun; others believe they respond to the magnetic pull of poles, as do simple compasses.

Pigeons are strongly territorial and defend their nests bravely against intruders, including other pigeons and even human hands that might threaten their offspring. Male pigeons love to strut proudly and sing a rhythmic *"hoo-bok bok"* song to impress nearby females. But pigeons are monogamous and will dedicate themselves indefinitely to a chosen mate. Mates are gentle and attentive with each other, grooming each other's necks, resting near each other, flying together, and locking beaks in a gesture that reminds most humans of kissing.

A photograph of Andualem Minale,
an Ethiopian boy who inspired
the writing of this story.